Be kind, Be cool, Be You

善良，酷，做自己

幸福人生的188个信条，如果曾有人告诉我这些就好了

[英] 妮基 · 迈尔斯 著/绘　喻之晓 译

中信出版集团 | 北京

图书在版编目（CIP）数据

善良，酷，做自己：汉英对照 /（英）妮基·迈尔斯著绘；喻之晓译. -- 北京：中信出版社，2021.5（2024.4 重印）

书名原文：Be kind, be cool, be you:inspiring words to live your life

ISBN 978-7-5217-2851-4

Ⅰ. ①善… Ⅱ. ①妮… ②喻… Ⅲ. ①儿童故事—图画故事—英国—现代 Ⅳ. ① I561.85

中国版本图书馆 CIP 数据核字 (2021) 第 034064 号

善良，酷，做自己

著 绘 者：[英] 妮基 · 迈尔斯
译　　者：喻之晓
出版发行：中信出版集团股份有限公司
（北京市朝阳区东三环北路27号嘉铭中心　邮编　100020）
承 印 者：北京盛通印刷股份有限公司

开　　本：787mm × 1092mm　1/24　　印　　张：8
京权图字：01-2021-1808　　字　　数：86千字
版　　次：2021年5月第1版　　印　　次：2024年4月第12次印刷
书　　号：ISBN 978-7-5217-2851-4
定　　价：68.00元

出　　品：中信儿童书店
图书策划：知学园
策划编辑：姜晓娜　韩晗
责任编辑：温慧　孙婧媛
营销编辑：姚梦云　王晓
装帧设计：谢佳静　　内文排版：谢佳静

服务热线：400-600-8099
投稿邮箱：author@citicpub.com

如果
曾有人
告诉我这些
就好了

你的梦想一定会实现

You can achieve your dreams

你笑起来真好看

Smile, it SUITS you

Throw
Kindness around
like Confetti

像抛出五彩纸屑一样
把爱撒播四方

你本来就
很棒

YOU
are cool
just
the way
you are

Self-belief is
a superpower
自信的力量无穷大

你的未来绚烂多彩

Your future is so bright and colourful

When it rains, look for rainbows

下雨时，别忘了寻找彩虹

Keep GOING, KEEP growing

努力前行，努力成长

保持活力
PROTECT
your
ENERGY

想法并不代表事实
Thoughts are NOT FACTS

那么多人
爱着你
YOU are SO
lOVed

别怕不完美和混乱
Don't be afraid
to be imperfect
and messy

相信自己的能力

Believe in your own abilities

your flaws make you unique and awesome

缺点让你与众不同

Remember to tell yourself you're doing great

记得告诉自己，你很棒

START EACH DAY WITH A GRATEFUL HEART

用感恩的心开启每一天

好事一定会发生

good THINGS will happen

成功有时不一定
来得那么快

success
doesn't
have to be
instant

跟别人不一样很酷

Being different is COOL

Follow
your own Path
走自己的路

哭泣不等于软弱

crying is not a weakness

Turn your dreams into plans

把梦想落实到计划上

照顾好自己

Take care of yourself

你不可能永远
让所有人满意

It's impossible to
please everyone
all the time

每个人都有自己的路

Everyone is on their own journey

像超级明星一样，发光吧！

Keep shining like a superstar

It's never too late to turn over a new leaf
重新开始永远不晚

Have the courage to be yourself

勇敢做自己

一千个人眼里
有一千种完美
Perfect is different
for everybody

The magic
is in YOU
你，可以
创造奇迹

大大的梦

DREAM BIG

任何时候都不要忘记
表达你的善意
It's always a good time to be kind

保持乐观是头等大事
POSITIVITY IS KEY

偶尔做个白日梦吧

DON'T QUIT YOUR DAY DREAM

不跟他人比较

stop comparing yourself to everyone else

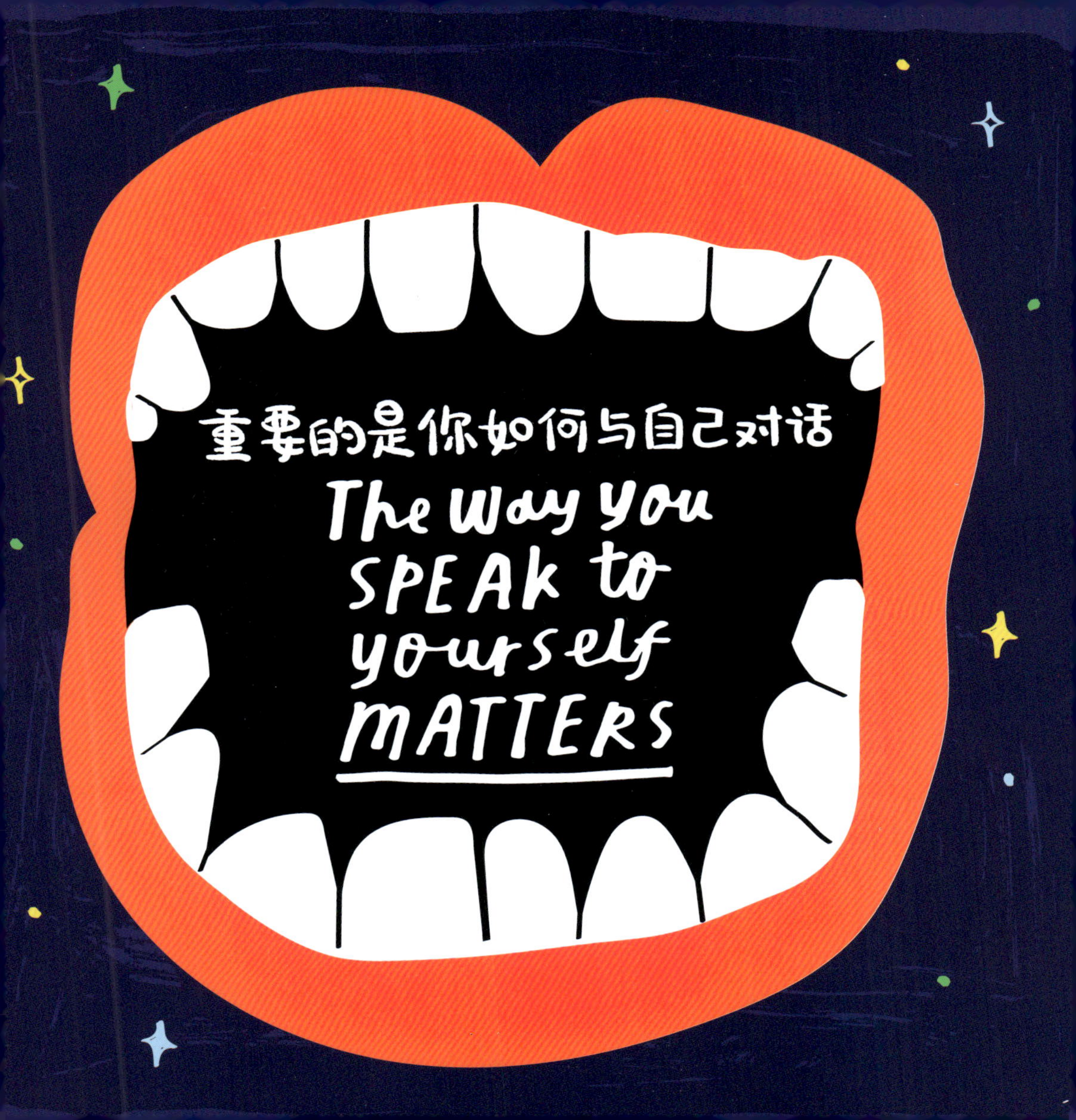
重要的是你如何与自己对话
The Way you SPEAK to yourself MATTERS

帮助他人
就是成就自己

We rise by
lifting up
others

You deserve love and happiness

你值得所有的爱和快乐

Don't be hard on yourself

别对自己太苛刻

Believe that you CAN
相信自己，你可以

别把
自己的感受
封藏起来
Don't Bottle up
your feelings

你让世界变得更精彩

YOU MAKE THE WORLD A COLOURFUL PLACE

与众不同
是件好事

Being unique is a good thing

偶尔感到迷茫
也没关系
It's ok to
feel lost
sometimes

创造你想要的生活
GROW a LIFE
that you
WANT to
LIVE

小小的进步
也好过原地踏步

Slow Progress is better
than NO PROGRESS

为你取得的进步
感到骄傲

BE PROUD OF
HOW FAR YOU'VE COME

It's Ok to tell someone you trust when you're not feeling ok

心情不好时
找个信任的人聊聊

我相信我自己

I Believe in myself

多一点儿善意，少一点儿评判

A little more kindness, a little less judgement

你真好啊
You are so sweet

Let go of things that make you unhappy

忘记那些不开心的事吧

kindness
is NOT a
weakness
善良不等于软弱

you don't have to prove anything to anyone

你不需要向任何人证明任何事情

你的潜能无限大

Your potential is never-ending

每个人都有难过的时候
EVERYBODY has SAD days

你能行
YOU CAN
DO THIS

对自己诚实一点儿

BE TRUE TO YOURSELF

Done is BETTER than perfect

完成比完美更重要

It's not your job to please everyone

你不需要取悦任何人

It's OK to NOT do EVERYTHING

没有尽善尽美
也没有关系

You are stronger and smarter than you think

你比自己想象的更强大、更聪明

SELF-Care
is NOT
selfish
爱自己不等于自私

Give yourself SPACE
给自己留点儿空间

善待身边的每一个人
Share kindness
with everyone

You are beautiful, kind and strong

你是如此
美丽、善良和强大

ALLOW yourself to GROW

给自己时间去成长

Don't dim your light to please other people

不要为了取悦他人而委屈自己

Keep your EYES on your OWN PATH
专心走自己的路

在哪里扎根
就在哪里绽放
BLOOM
WHERE YOU are
Planted

YOU ARE
ENOUGH
做自己，就够了

KINDness
IS FREE
善意无价

在一个可以选择的世界里
选择做一个善良的人

In a World
WHERE YOU
CAN Be
Anything,
BE KIND

即使没有让所有人满意，也没关系

YOU CAN'T PLEASE EVERYONE AND THAT'S OKAY

你不必隐藏
自己的感受
you don't
HAVE to
hide the
way you
FEEL

SURROUND yourself with PEOPLE who FEEL LIKE sunshine
与阳光般
温暖的人在一起

唯有行动能让梦想成真

DREAMS
ONLY WORK
IF YOU DO

Always give a little more kindness than is expected

让别人的期待，多满足一点点

生命太短，要多爱自己

Life is too short to not love yourself

你的价值不在于
拥有多少粉丝，收获多少赞

Likes and Follows do NOT
define your self-WORTH

make your own MAGIC

创造属于自己的奇迹

Life is SHORT so do what makes you HAPPY and surround yourself with nice PEOPLE

生命很短，
所以要做
快乐的事，
结交
美好的人

做错了也没关系

It's OK to make mistakes

每一天都是新的开始
every day
is a fresh
start

尽力就够了

Your best is always good enough

你值得被爱，
被尊重，被善待
you deserve lots of
self-love, respect
and kindness

SURROUND YOURSELF WITH PEOPLE WHO 'GET IT'

和懂你的人在一起

You are allowed to change your mind

试试换一个思路

Be kind Online
在网上也要对人友善

Flowers don't grow without rain

不经历风雨，
就没有鲜花盛开

Life is a miracle and so are you

生命是奇迹，你也是

you are a shining light on the darkest days

你是灰暗岁月里的一束亮光

Being rejected doesn't mean you're not good enough

被拒绝并不意味着你不够好

Be Proud of your progress

为自己的每一点进步而自豪

it's OK if you feel sad for no reason

莫名地心情低落
也很正常

You can say NO and still be a nice person

好人也可以说"不"

Someone else's success isn't your FAILURE

别人的成功

并不意味着你的失败

你比你想象的更勇敢

You're braver than you believe

记住，你的感受最重要

Remember that your feelings matter

温柔地对自己说话，
就像温柔地对朋友说话一样

Speak kindly to yourself like you would to a friend

不要为无法掌控的事焦虑

Stop worrying about things out of your control

你的善意能给他人力量

Being Kind gives Others STRENGTH

Do something that scares you a little bit every day

每天都可以尝试一些以前不敢做的事情

Be kind to people who are different from you

善待那些跟你不一样的人

Choose kindness over judgement

多一点儿宽容，少一点儿评判

Strong People lift Other People Up

强大的人可以激励他人

Be the reason
someone
smiles today
今天，让某个人因你而露出笑脸

You don't have to apologise for being yourself

你不必为做自己而道歉

Be kind to your mind

善待自己的内心

If you're looking for a positive sign, this is it

如果你在寻找转机，
那么转机已经握在手中

偶尔不在状态也没关系

It's Ok to go Offline for a While

You're not letting anyone down
你没有让任何人失望

Love always wins

爱无往而不胜

The world needs your kind heart

世界需要你的爱心

kind people are my kind of people

与善良的人同行

your mind is powerful

你的内心无比强大

If you don't have anything kind to say, don't say anything at all

如果你不想说善意的话，那就什么都别说

Always listen to others, with a loving heart

永远心怀爱意，倾听他人心声

Don't let yesterday's troubles ruin today

别让昨天的烦恼
毁了今天的心情

我们都能用
自己的方式
让这个世界变得
更美好

We can all make a
difference
in our own way

Be happy in the moment

快乐在每一个当下

Your voice matters
你的意见很重要

不是只有擅长
才能乐在其中

You don't have to
be good at something
to enjoy it

DO What makes your soul sparkle

做让心灵
闪闪发亮的事

This is a good day to have a good day

努力让每一天
都成为美好的一天

Let yourself rest

累了就休息一下

Change can be beautiful

变化可以很美妙

use your talents to do good

把才华用在对的地方

Love the life that you have right now

当下即美好

It's not always about the destination, it's about the journey

重要的不总是结果，
而是过程

Be the POSitive energy that you want to attract

成为你想要的那束光

Being yourself is your super POWER

你最好的样子
就是做自己

Find the magic in tiny moments of joy

每个快乐的瞬间都隐藏着魔力

From a tiny seed
grows a mighty tree
一粒小小的种子
也会长成参天大树

It's OK to take one step at a time
一次进步一点点就很好

Be a colourful rainbow on a stormy day

在风雨交加的日子里
做一道绚丽的彩虹

It's Ok to put your needs first sometimes

有时候，要学会把自己的需求放在第一位

Love your-self
好好爱自己

When people support each other, amazing things can happen

相互帮助可以创造奇迹

You have totally got this

你一定没问题

寻求帮助不丢人

Asking for help isn't failure

Life is not a competition

生活不是一场比赛

Nothing is impossible

一切皆有可能

say yes to things that make you happy

拥抱让你快乐的一切

Cloudy days always pass

阴霾总会过去

If you can't find the sunshine, be the sunshine

找不到阳光，
就成为阳光

Be a friend
to someone
that needs one

有谁需要朋友
就做他的朋友吧

use your voice
to be heard
让世界听到你的声音

Don't hold on to sad thoughts for too long
别让悲伤停留太久

GOOd things take time

好事多磨

Everyone has slower days and that's OK
没关系，谁都有挣扎的时候

Have an
attitude
of gratitude

要有一颗感恩的心

Forgive yourself for past mistakes

原谅曾经犯错的自己

乌云的背后是蓝天

Behind every grey cloud is a sunny blue sky

伸出手
去摘星星
Reach
for the
stars

Rise AND SUNSHINE
起床，去燃烧你的小宇宙

It's ok if you don't know all of the answers

不知道所有答案也没关系

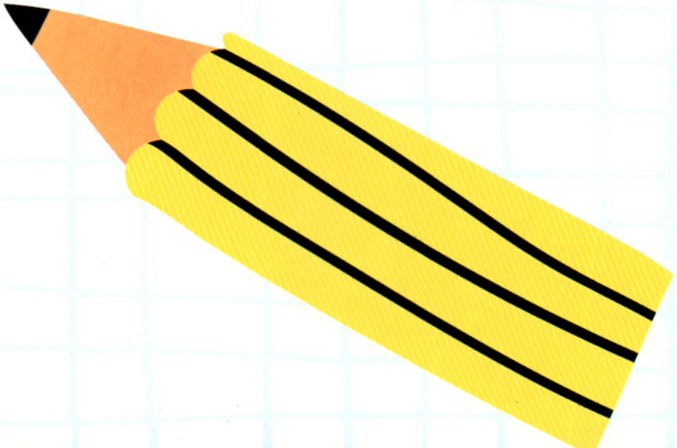

每次进步一点点，
小成就也会带来大改变

Tiny bits of progress add up to big results

Don't worry if a few people don't like you

即使有一些人不喜欢你，
也没关系

You can bloom through sunshine and storms
暑往寒来，我自盛开

some days can be tough, but so are you

生活有时艰难，而你坚不可摧

你不知道自己有多棒

Don't underestimate how amazing you are

You can be happy for other people
without questioning
your own achievements

为别人高兴，也肯定自己

You are capable of amazing things

你可以创造奇迹

You can do anything you put your mind to

只要用心，没有做不到的事

No one belongs in this world more than you do
你是独一无二的存在，
没有谁可以取代

Everybody fails before they succeed

不经历风雨，怎么见彩虹

Focus on your happy thoughts

专注于那些让你快乐的想法

It's Ok to ask for help even if you think others have it worse than you

即使情况并不是很糟，你也可以向别人求助

Every body
is a work
in progress

每个人都在不断成长

It's ok to go at your own pace
按自己的节奏前进就好啊

善待别人是最伟大的艺术
The greatest art is treating people with kindness

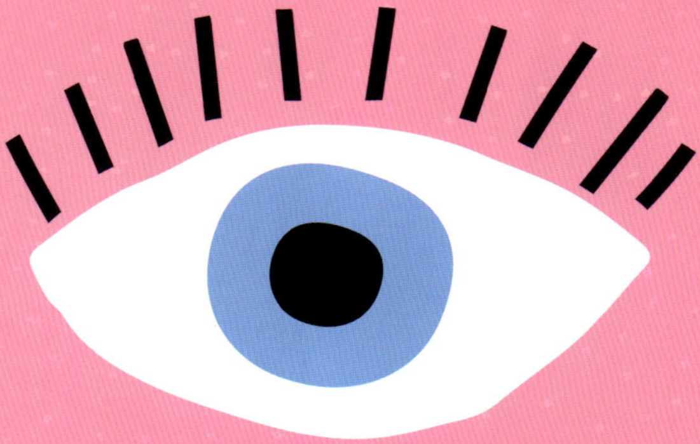

LOOK for the good in all things

发现每件事的积极面

为每一次
小小的进步而欢呼
Celebrate
every tiny
triumph

You deserve every compliment
你值得所有称赞

You are
a ray of
sunshine

你就是
一道阳光

妮基·迈尔斯（*Nikki Miles*）

英国新锐插画家，与未婚夫马特（Matt）和毛茸茸的英国蓝猫卢娜（Luna）一起生活在伦敦。妮基喜欢用色彩丰富的插图和手绘字向世界传播积极和友善的话语。从拿起画笔的那一天起，妮基就没有停止过绘画，也无法想象没有它的生活。她喜欢画画，只是因为它能为某个人的一天增添些明媚。她的工作灵感来自日常生活中的经历和感受、户外活动、书籍、电影、时尚，以及20世纪中叶的设计、复古包装和广告等。妮基业余时间喜欢读书、散步、摄影和学习书法。